WAVE THE FLAG AND BLOW THE WHISTLE

For Joss and Tomas who loved trains

R.A.

For Mum and Dad

A.G.

EGMONT

We bring stories to life

First published in Great Britain 2012
by Egmont UK Limited
239 Kensington High Street
London W8 6SA

www.egmont.co.uk

Text copyright © Ronda Armitage 2012
Illustrations copyright © Andrew Gordon 2012

The moral rights of the author and illustrator have been asserted

ISBN 978 1 4052 5339 0 (Hardback)
ISBN 978 1 4052 5340 6 (Paperback)

1 3 5 7 9 10 8 6 4 2

A CIP catalogue record for this title is available from the British Library

Printed and bound in Singapore

47117/1/2

WAVE THE FLAG AND BLOW THE WHISTLE

Ronda Armitage ✦ Andrew Gordon

EGMONT

"Ready, Tom, ready?"

"Ready, Grandpa, ready.

"To Blueberry Hill,

to Blueberry Hill.

We're catching the train

to Blueberry Hill."

"I'm ready too," says Spotty Raffe.

Oh dear, nobody hears him.

Grandpa and Tom

trittity trot,

trittity trot to the station.

"What about me?"

calls Spotty Raffe.

And he goes galloping after.

"Tickets, please! Tickets, please!"

LOOK!

An express train travelling fast.

Who-o-osh!

Here's the train to Blueberry Hill,

the train for Tom and Grandpa.

"Ready, Tom, ready?"

"Ready, Grandpa, ready!"

No! No! *The train musn't go.*

Look outside!

Who is galloping? Who? Who?

Spotty Raffe is coming too.

Hurry, hurry all aboard.

Wave the flag and blow the whistle.

Poop! Poop! Chuggity chug.

Going faster, swishing by.

Look outside.

An orange tractor, with four fat pigs.

A yellow digger dig, dig, digs.

Look inside.

Spotty Raffe sees Nellie Phant.

"Hurry, hurry," says the train.

Chuggity chug, chuggity chug.

Into a tunnel dark as night.

Who-O-o, who-O-o.

Who is scared?

Who is hiding, eyes shut tight?

"Hurry, hurry," says the train.

Choggity chog, choggity chog.

Out of the tunnel, into the light.

Look outside.

There is a river, three boats and a crane,

cars on a road and a freight train.

Look inside.

Spotty Raffe and Tom play

with Nellie Phant and Maisie.

One Granny and one Grandpa

share a nice cup of tea.

"Blueberry Hill, this is Blueberry Hill.

Everyone off for Blueberry Hill."

Crying and laughing.

Rushing and pushing.

"Wait for me!"
calls Spotty Raffe.

"Where's Spotty Raffe?"

says Grandpa.

Oh train,

don't go, don't go!

Look, look there he is.

Spotty Raffe, hello, hello!

"I'm the grand old Duke of York," says Tom.

"So am I," says Maisie.

We'll all march up to the top of the hill.

And we'll all march down again.

Time to go home now,

time to go home.

Ready, train, ready?

Ready, everyone, ready?

Wave the flag and

blow the whistle.

But oh no, the train won't go.

Ping, ping

Dong, dong

No, no, this train won't go.

Everyone out at the station.

The guard on the platform goes

ring, ring, ring.

The children on the platform

run,   *run,*   *run.*

The babies on the platform
chuckle, chuckle, chuckle.

Tom and Maisie
throw, throw, throw.

Spotty Raffe and Nellie Phant dingle-dangle-down-oh.

A **squeal**

and a **who-o-osh-sh-sh**,

and a **poop, poop, poop.**

Another train at the station.

Tom waves the flag.

Maisie blows the whistle.

"All aboard, all aboard."

This train is ready.

hee-hee-hee.

Catch

No, *no, don't go, don't go.*

Tom and Maisie . . .

What can they see?

Two passengers dangling

down from a tree.

hem
if
you
can
and hold them tight.

This train

is ready to go.

Slow, slow, slowly s l o w.

Look inside.

Tom and Maisie close their eyes.

Hushity hush, hushity hush.

Look outside.

Stars in the sky,

while the moon stands still

over Blueberry Hill.